OFF
TO THE
RACES

By
Fred and Marjorie Phleger

Illustrated by
Leo Summers

BEGINNER BOOKS   A Division of Random House, Inc.

A   B   C   D   E   F   G   H   I   J   K
1   2   3   4

My brother, Bob, is a bike racer.

I like to watch him ride.

He wins many races.

I wish I could race too.

Bob rides every day.
Sometimes he lets me
ride with him.

"I want to race too," I tell him.
But he just laughs and says,
"You're too young, kid."

He thinks I'm too young.
Someday I'll show him.
I'll show him that I can race!

Tonight Bob is getting ready
to go to a bike rally.
It will take him two days to ride there.
"Why can't I go to the rally?" I ask him.

"A two-day trip is too far for you.
You'd slow me up," he says.

When Bob goes to bed,

I look at his map.

It's just a little two-day trip.

If he can do it, so can I!

It is morning.

Bob is going.

"Too bad you can't come," he says.

"You're just too young."

Mom and Dad wave good-bye.
But I don't wave.

Bob doesn't know it,
but I am going, too.

I don't care how far it is.

I'm not afraid of a long trip.

I am going to follow Bob.

I am going to go
to that rally!

I'm on my way.

This is easy.

This road is getting hilly.

This is hard work.

It won't be long.

I'll catch up with Bob soon.

I think I'll stop
and rest awhile.

Oh-oh! A bear!
I'm lucky he's after honey
and not after me.

I've got to get out of here fast!
I've got to get back on the road!

Now it's raining.

Bob was right.

This is a long, hard trip.

Maybe I should have stayed home.

What a muddy road!
I have to push my bike.

I hope I can get to
that building up there.
It may be the hostel
where Bob is sleeping tonight.

Yes, this is the place.

I see Bob's bike.

I open the door.

Bob yells at me,

"What are YOU doing here?

You'll have to go home."

But then Bob sees how wet I am.

"You dumb kid," he says.

"Get out of your clothes.

Get into bed.

You'll have to sleep here tonight."

Later I hear him talking to Dad.
"The kid is with me. He's okay.
I'll take him along
to the rally tomorrow."

In the morning we clean up the hostel.

"Now listen, kid," Bob tells me,

"I'm taking you to the rally.

But you'll have to ride fast.

You'll have to keep up with me."

We ride all day long.
We meet other riders
going to the rally.
By afternoon I'm tired,
but we're almost there.

We will be here two nights.

We will sleep in tents.

We eat outside.

I'm hungry after our long ride.

The rally begins right after supper.

The first thing is the Night Ride.

It is a short ride.

The big fun begins tomorrow.

In the morning there are
all kinds of bike games.
Some are very hard.
Some are sort of crazy.

The first game
is a Slalom Race.
Bob wins it.
I knew he would.

Next comes the Wiggly Board Race.
Most riders are afraid of this one.

But Bob can ride his bike on anything.
I hope he will win this, too.

He does!

He wins it!

Bob is first again!

It's fun to watch Bob
win these races.
But I sure wish
that I could race, too.

After lunch we see the Cycle Circus.

What a show!

High wheelers! Low wheelers!

One wheelers! Three wheelers!

And one big bike

that holds a whole family!

Races and games all day long!
Every few minutes
a new one starts.

Everyone is in a race or game.
I wish I could be in something.

Late in the day Bob surprises me.

"Hey, kid, want to race?

We've set up a Kids' Race," he says.

"Come on, get your bike ready."

Hooray, I'm going to be in a race!

I put on a race helmet.

Bob checks my bike for me.

We're on the line. Ready to go!

I know the others are good riders.

I hope I can keep up with them.

"Take it easy, kid," Bob says.
"All you have to do
is follow the arrows."

The first arrow points up a hill.
A muddy hill! A bumpy hill!
One kid can't make it.
He has to push his bike.
But I'm all right.
I keep going up.

A new arrow points to a wall.

We have to pull our bikes over it.

If they want us to do it . . .

well, I'll do it!

Now we have to ride through water.

One kid falls in.

I hope I don't fall.

I want to win this race!

But there's someone ahead of me.

I try and try,

but I can't catch him.

I come in second.

I hear Bob yelling,
"Good race, kid!
Maybe you didn't win,
but now you really are a racer!"

The rally is almost over.
This is our last night.
We all parade on our bikes
around a bonfire.
We all have fun showing off.

In the morning, Bob and I
wave good-bye to our friends.
"We'll see them next year," Bob says.
"Because next year you're coming back.
And next year you're going to win."